# ONCE UPON A MAGIC NIGHT

## BY JOHN A. PETERSON

This book is a work of fiction. Any references to real people, events, establishments, organizations, or locales are intended solely to provide a sense of authenticity and are used fictitiously. All other characters, incidents, and dialogue are drawn from the author's imagination and are not to be construed as real.

Roger + Lorraine

May you always have

love + magic!

your friend

John

# DEDICATION

I dedicate this story to my wife, Nikki, whose love and encouragement make every day magic.

# TABLE OF CONTENTS

PROLOGUE                                      9

MY FIRST MAGIC NIGHT                         14

THE NEXT MORNING                             25

LATER THAT AFTERNOON                         36

A PROPER CUP OF TEA                          38

IN THE TENT                                  41

THE FINAL ACT                                45

INTO THE NIGHT                               48

MISCHA'S STORY                               50

OUR WORST DAY EVER                           54

THE STRANGE BUILDING                         59

OUR FIRST PERFORMANCE AND A NEW LIFE    62

ONE DOOR CLOSES                              65

BACK IN THE TRAILER                          72

THE ENCOUNTER                                74

WHEN EVERYTHING CHANGED                      83

# PROLOGUE

It was a moonless night that found Sgt. Finley leading his squad down a narrow, winding trail in the central mountains of a Middle Eastern country in a region fought over for thousands of years. Tonight their mission was to rescue a teenage boy from insurgents who had kidnapped and held him for ransom or they would kill him. This boy was the son of a tribal leader who had crossed swords with the insurgents and was loyal to the Americans. The mission was called Operation Ten Pin, just like in bowling, where you have to pick up the elusive ten pin.

# ONCE UPON A MAGIC NIGHT

Finn, as he liked to be called, knew that this was a dangerous mission but one for which he and his men were trained. Dressed in camouflage gear and in possession of some new high-tech weapons, these men were ready for anything.

Finn saw a cluster of mud huts about two hundred meters directly ahead. There were dim lights coming through the windows of the largest hut. Finn pointed to this one as their target for tonight.

As Finn approached the front of the hut, his men took up their positions. Finn heard each man give a short chirp that mimicked the local songbirds. They were ready. Finn put in his earplugs and he was just about ready too.

He reached into the side pocket of his fatigues. His fingers caressed a round metal object just a little larger than a golf ball. He pulled it out of his pocket. This was a *screamer*. He had used them before in training and he had been impressed how well they worked.

A screamer was one of the new weapons the military was using to confuse and control the enemy. It gave off a very high pitch whine that incapacitated anyone in its vicinity. The only defense against a screamer was a set of special sound-deadening military issue earplugs.

He knocked on the door. A young man with a beard,

turban and flowing robe opened the door partway not expecting to see an American soldier dressed in camouflage fatigues and face darkened with charcoal.

Finn spoke perfectly in the local dialect, Hazaragi, "Good Evening! I have a special present from the great white father" and with that Finn tossed the armed screamer past the young man into the hut.

One-two-three seconds and EEEEEEEEEE-EEEEEEEEEE the screamer was activated. Finn kicked the door open. Several men sitting on the floor clutched their ears hoping to stop the piercing sound tearing into their brains.

Finn looked around the room and then in the far corner crouching on the floor was a young man, a teenage boy, who matched the description given to Finn. He grabbed the kid by the arm and together they ran outside the hut. The teenage boy was terrified. He thought it was bad enough being held captive and he sure didn't know what was going to happen next!

Once outside, a bullet whizzed by Finn's head. One of the insurgents was hopelessly trying to pull off a shot at him but couldn't aim properly. The boy and Finn ran as fast as they could to a couple of large boulders for cover. Finn tugged on the kid's arm to make him sit down. The boy crouched down and asked, "What is going on? Where are you taking me? Where is my father?"

Finn told him to sit down and not to make a sound. He looked into the boy's eyes and saw someone who was totally lost and confused. Finn wished this kid wasn't here and was somewhere else safe, doing what teenage kids do in this God-forsaken country. Instead, he was just a pawn.

For a second, Finn felt a connection with this innocent young man. He thought he could have been friends with the boy when Finn was a teenager back home before his parents died and he joined the Army.

Then something went wrong. The kid stood up and started shouting, "I'm here, I'm here." Finn lunged at the boy but before he could pull him down, one lucky shot hit the boy in the head and down he went. The kid didn't look good.

Another bullet came pretty close to Finn. He unclipped his EL-250, Electronic Laser Gun, from his belt and set it on the *fireworks* mode. Finn pointed it straight up in the air and fired one long burst. A beautiful, large fireworks ball illuminated the sky one hundred feet above the hut. What followed was a sizzling-like sound and then nothing for a few seconds.

## ONCE UPON A MAGIC NIGHT

Finn and the other members of his squad knew what was coming next, so they tipped their heads down and covered their eyes. The enemy fighters were now standing outside the hut and they looked up to see if there was going to be more fireworks. The last thing these men would ever see was the brightest light on earth, a scorching blue-white light that seared their retinas and fried their optic nerve endings. They were instantly blinded for the rest of their lives. They would now be officially classified as non-combatants.

Finn and his men stood over the young boy's limp body. For all the missions he had been on and for all his successes and failures, this one really got to him. The others in the squad looked at Finn and asked him if he was okay. Finn was unusually quiet. He looked down at the boy and choked, "Damn it, kid. Damn it."

# MY FIRST MAGIC NIGHT

I guess you could call me a night owl. I've always liked doing things at night ever since I was a kid. When you compare nighttime to daytime; the air smells different, the people are different and your activities are totally different than what you'd experience during the day.

I always liked to sleep during the day and then once the sun would set, I'd get up and live my life. I was more alive at night than I could ever be during the day.

I'll always remember the night when I cruised into a little town on the edge of the Mojave Desert on my 1967 Triumph Bonneville motorcycle. The Bonneville had been my only transportation since getting out of the Army and I really enjoyed how she handled. She was a classic and in very good condition. To me she was worth a million bucks.

The old gentlemen who sold me the bike knew Johnny Allen who raced at Bonneville in 1953 and clocked 193 mph on such a machine. Every mile I put on the Bonny was a step back in history.

My theory of life is the more things you have the harder it is to leave. So I tried to keep life simple, I only needed the basics.

I had been wandering through the southwest for the better part of a year. After my discharge from the Army, I didn't know what I was looking for in my life. But I kept on moving and searching. I felt that as long as I kept trying, I'd find what I was looking for.

It was about nine o'clock at night. I was having a cup of coffee and a piece of pie at the only coffee shop on the main drag of this little town. I looked up from my pie and saw a large motor home drive by the coffee shop. On the side of the motor home was a sign that caught my attention, "Come See the World's Greatest Magic Show." On the sign were shooting stars and people performing various stunts and magic, like floating in the air, and parlor tricks.

Following the first motor home was a caravan of vehicles loaded with all kinds of equipment. The vehicles turned into the parking lot just past the coffee shop and stopped. I watched as people stepped out of their vehicles and gathered together. I tried not to be too obvious, but I kept looking at these people. I was curious to see who they were.

I have always enjoyed magic shows. Ever since childhood, I'd watch real close to try to figure out how a magic trick was done and then I'd attempt to duplicate it. Magicians always impressed me, how they could entertain the audience and how they made their tricks look so easy.

A short, heavy-set man stepped out of the driver's side of the first motor home; a woman came out of the other side and stood next to him. They started talking. She had jet black hair, olive skin and a smile that drew me in like an attractive flower draws a honey bee to sample its nectar! These two people were talking intently as the others in their group came up to them. He pointed to the café and they looked right at me as I was looking back at them. I kept staring at the woman; she was beautiful.

Moments later the group entered the coffee shop

which was pretty busy even at this time of night. The heavy-set man and the woman looked in my direction. There were a couple of seats empty at my table, so I waved at them to come and join me.

As they approached, the man stuck out his hand and announced in an English accent, "Good evening, Sir! Thanks ever so much for sharing your table with us. Teddy's the name. This is Mischa."

I stood up and shook his outstretched hand. I reached out to Mischa to shake her hand as well and tried to clear my throat. "My name is Robert Finley but my friends call me Finn. It's nice to meet you. Please, have a seat and tell me about your magic show."

Teddy offered the first chair to Mischa. He waved his hand over the chair and it began to move out from the table. Mischa sat down on the chair. Teddy waved his hand again over the chair and Mischa sitting in the chair moved up to the table. He never touched the chair! Needless to say, I was impressed with his trick. This happened so casually that it seemed like I was the only one to notice what he had just done. With a big grin on my face I nodded to Teddy. He smiled back.

Sitting across from me, they told me that they travelled from small town to small town entertaining people with their magic tricks. They had been doing this for a while and enjoyed performing.

I told them that I had been wandering around the southwest on my motorcycle after getting out of the Army. I had been in the latest war and found it difficult to adjust to civilian life and working and living in one place just didn't interest me. I would stay a short time in a town and when I was bored, I would just move on.

I looked at Mischa; she looked back at me and for what seemed like an awkward moment or two we kept looking into each other's eyes. I felt like time had stopped. I had to shake my head to get back and focus on what Teddy was saying.

Teddy told me that he understood how I felt about travelling. He too had been wandering, not sure about his life but when he joined up with the magic show he felt that he was home. He said it must have been what he was looking for because he had been in the show for a few years now and didn't have any plans to leave.

I was wondering if Teddy and Mischa were "a couple". Even though she was sitting next to him, they didn't show any signs of an intimate relationship. They appeared to be friends, nothing more. Anyway that's what I assumed and that made me feel better.

# ONCE UPON A MAGIC NIGHT

The waitress came up to our table and asked what my guests would like to have. They ordered two cups of coffee and pie to go with it.

A friend of theirs who was sitting at one of the other tables came up hurriedly to Teddy and announced, "Sorry to bother you Teddy but it looks like someone is trying to get into your motor home!"

Teddy replied, "Thanks. I'll take care of it."

He got up and told us, "Enjoy your coffee and pie. It should only take a minute and I'll be right back."

Watching Teddy walking away from the table, I had a feeling that I should go with him. I hadn't told them that I had been in Special Ops in the Army and had been in some pretty tough fights. At that moment I felt the hair on the back of my neck go straight up, just like when I had been in those situations. I thought that I should probably follow him outside. There's nothing like having a little extra help if and when you need it.

I jumped up and stepped quickly to catch up. He sure could walk fast.

"Teddy, I'll go with you."

"No bother, we've had this before in these small towns. Sometimes folks just get curious and I would rather they come to our show tomorrow night."

Despite his air of confidence, I went along anyway. We headed out to the parking lot where their vehicles were. I saw a raised-up four wheel drive truck with a rebel flag painted on the driver's door. It was parked next to Teddy's motor home. Two overweight guys with shaved heads and wearing dirty blue jeans and sleeveless shirts were walking around Teddy's motor home. They were examining it closely and trying to peer into the windows.

As we approached these two guys, Teddy called out, "Hey, chaps. Would you like to come and see our show? Tomorrow night we'll be at the end of town. We have the large field reserved and I'll give you a couple of tickets."

One of the red-necks answered in a well-liquored up voice, "Nah. We want to see whatcha got in there."

Then the other red-neck added, "Yeah, ya' got any beer in there?"

I tensed up and prepared to give these punks an ass-whupping. These guys were bigger than both of us, but I figured that working together, we could probably take them on; they looked like they were pretty drunk.

I looked over at Teddy. In a calm voice he said, "Please step away from our motor home. Maybe you should go home now."

# ONCE UPON A MAGIC NIGHT

They were so wasted they were swaying back and forth. I thought for a second that Teddy and I were going to have to jump these guys and I wondered why none of Teddy's friends came out to help us.

Teddy calmly walked up to one of the red-necks and what happened next I can still remember in exact detail.

First, the red-neck closest to the motor home began to climb the small ladder on the back, ignoring Teddy's request to back away. He was reaching for the supplies on the top of the motor home, when Teddy raised his arms and cupped his hands like he was holding something between them. This red-neck looked back at Teddy with a puzzled look on his face.

Teddy blew air into his cupped hands. I heard a loud boom. It sounded like the sound-barrier breaking. What came out the other side of his hands was a strong gust of wind that was directed at the first red-neck. The red-neck was slammed by this force and was shot back like a freight train had hit him. He landed about thirty feet away, square on his butt.

Just then the second red-neck started towards Teddy. Teddy turned to face him and once again he blew into his cupped hands. I heard the same boom as the first time; the only difference was he directed the force at this guy's feet. This red-neck found his feet had been blown out from underneath him and he made two perfectly executed forward spins and then hit the ground facedown!

In about five seconds, both of these men were rendered harmless by this amazing little man. The first good ol' boy started crying like a baby. He didn't know what hit him. The second man was out cold. Teddy came up to the first red neck, shook him and asked him if he could stand up. He nodded. Teddy helped him get into the truck.

I went over to the second guy and picked him up off the ground. He was now coming to and shaking. He begged not to be harmed again.

"Don't you think it's about time you and your friend headed home?"

"Yeah!"

We loaded the second red-neck into the truck and watched them drive out of the parking lot and down the street and we started back to the coffee shop. I looked over at Teddy and asked him, "What the hell did you just do?"

"My friend, I will tell you what you saw, but for now just keep it to yourself. Please!"

With all that had just happened, it seemed to me like we had been gone for a long time. When, in fact, it had only been a few minutes.

We reentered the coffee shop. Teddy's friends gave us nods of approval and turned back to talking amongst themselves. The rest of the patrons didn't even look at us as we walked to our table.

Teddy and I sat back down. The waitress came to our table and refilled our coffees.

Mischa looked so soft and warm as she leaned towards me. She smelled good, like a field of desert flowers. A smell you'd never forget.

"Thank you Finn for going with Teddy and making sure no one got hurt." For a second I didn't know if she was making fun of me or really thanking me for going out there with Teddy.

I mumbled, "It was nothing." I thought that sounded stupid. Why do I say the lamest things around people I want to impress, especially this woman?

We finished our food, paid the waitress, and headed out the door. I didn't want to leave these people, but I didn't know what else to say. Thankfully, I didn't have to.

Teddy said, "Finn, would you like to camp with us? Tomorrow we're going to set up our tent and equipment.

We sure could use your help. Our first show will be tomorrow night."

Wow, I was ecstatic. "Yeah, that would be great! I really want to see the magic show and maybe you could teach me a trick or two?"

He smiled and stuck out his hand and said, "We'd love to have you stay with us." We shook hands.

I liked Teddy. His handiwork behind the motor homes certainly got my attention and going with them would probably give me a chance to learn more and well have more time getting to know Mischa. So I figured that I could tag along and I could help watch over the troupe. Sure, having Mr. Amazing was security for them but he couldn't be everywhere at the same time. Besides, Mischa shouldn't be alone if trouble came back.

So I got on the Triumph and followed them to an open field on the edge of town. They parked their vehicles next to one another. I found some space next to Teddy and Mischa's motor home, parked the bike and set up my tent. I threw my sleeping bag inside the tent, crawled in it and was soon fast asleep and dreaming.

# THE NEXT MORNING

It was nice lying in my sleeping bag. I felt the warmth of the morning sun heat up my tent. I listened to the sounds of those around me getting up; I smelled the fresh coffee brewing and the breakfast cooking, which made me ready to get up. I realized my usual sleep cycle was really screwed up now.

After what I had seen last night my expectations were high about tonight's show. Questions were on my mind. How did he do that? Could he teach me too? What else was he capable of?

I got out of the tent and walked towards Teddy's

motor home, I had to attend to some bodily needs. Teddy was leaving his motor home and he looked at me and said, "Good morning, Finn. Sleep well? Would you like to use the bathroom?" I wondered if he could read minds too.

"Good morning, Teddy. Yes, sir. I slept better than ever last night. And, yes, I need to use the facilities."

He held the door to the motor home open and said, "Finn, please, go right in and make yourself at home."

I thanked him and walked in. At the far end of the motor home I saw a closed door. A small kid's-like sign was on the door. It said, "Mischa's Domain."

I started to open the door to the bathroom when I heard the "Mischa's Domain" door open. This lovely little woman was standing there in her pajamas, looking no worse for being asleep. Her hair was not in any disarray that I could tell. Her pajamas looked like she had just put them on. She looked great! I must have been staring when she said, "Would you like to use the bathroom first?"

I was stunned into silence. Here she was standing in front of me and I couldn't take my gaze off of her. She said, "Go on" and those words broke the spell she had on me.

After breakfast, Teddy explained what I could do to help them set up the tent. It sounded like I would be put to good use, lifting here and pulling there, as there were only a few men in the group. He said that they could really use an extra set of hands.

I thanked them for breakfast and headed back outside to put away my things. I folded up my tent and sleeping bag. I was placing them back on the bike when I saw a young boy from the group playing nearby. The boy could not have been more than four or five years old. He was quietly playing with some small objects on the ground. At first I didn't pay him any attention. Then something inside me told me to take a closer look at what he was doing.

"Hi, my name is Finn. What's yours?"

"My name is Joey."

I stood next to him and looked over his shoulder to see what he was playing with. Then my eyes must have gotten as big as the plates our pie was served on last night. Oh my God! The little objects Joey was playing with were floating in the air and changing shapes. He said, "Stop!" and the figures stopped in mid-air. He gave out a little boy's giggle and then commanded them to spin around and they started spinning. He said, "Be puppy dogs" and then they all were little dogs running around in a small circle barking chasing each other.

A slender, young woman came up behind us. She introduced herself, "My name's Sophie. I see you've met my son, Joey. He really likes his spinners."

"Yes, ma'am. He really does. My name's Finn."

We shook hands and continued watching Joey play with the spinners.

"These things are amazing. How do they work?"

"I don't know exactly, but Teddy does and I'm sure he can explain it to you. Tonight we'll have even larger ones in the Magic Show."

"What kind of magic do you perform?"

"I don't perform any magic. I help with the costumes and the equipment."

"Have you been with the group very long?"

"For a couple of years now, but excuse us, Joey and I have a lot of work to do to get everything ready for tonight. We'll see you later."

Sophie turned to Joey and asked him to stop playing and come with her. She told him he needed to help too. It was nice to see that everyone had a job to do, regardless of their age.

Joey held open his hand with the toy pieces in it and

showed them to me. They were just small pebbles, nothing more. He looked up at me and we smiled at each other. He stood up and ran to his mother. What a cute kid! And I loved those toys!

I turned around and saw Teddy leave his motor home. He must have seen me talking to Sophie and Joey.

"That looks like one more thing I'm going to have to explain to you by the look on your face. But first we need to set up the tent for tonight's performance."

I told him that sounded good and followed him to where everyone was gathering. There was a large canvas ball that was in the center of the field. This was the tent and Teddy was giving directions for everyone to begin unfolding it. Tent poles were being strategically placed seventy-five to one hundred feet from the canvas mound. Looking at the mound I didn't think the tent was going to be that big until we unrolled it. The more we unrolled, the bigger it became. I realized that this tent was going to be HUGE!

After a few minutes, we had shifted the canvas mound to the left and to the right. Then as we spread it out we had to straighten out the lumps in the canvas here and there. Now we were ready to raise the tent.

I had seen pictures of carnivals and circuses and their

tent raisings; they always had a crane or an elephant or something that could pull the great weight of the tent up in the air. I looked around and all I saw was people power. There were only a dozen men, women and children. No heavy lifting equipment anywhere.

Teddy and two other men walked to the middle of the canvas. They knelt down and grabbed handfuls of the tent material. But as they stood up they and the tent began to rise up in the air. I couldn't figure out how they did it, but I was sure impressed. These guys were just rising up in the air with the tent!

The rest of the group scurried around, propping up the tent with the tent poles and then they tied off each corner. This was truly an amazing thing to see! The show hadn't even started and I was witnessing magic.

If I hadn't seen this tent go up with my own eyes I never would have believed that it was the work of only a few people. OK, I had to sit down; this was too much for me to believe. Mischa came over to me. She put her hand on my shoulder.

"Are you OK, Finn?"

"No, I'm not OK. I saw Teddy fight two bullies last night in the parking lot by blowing gusts of air on them and knocking them to the ground. Then this morning I saw Joey playing with stones that changed shapes just by him telling them to change. And now I saw the way you raised the tent by just lifting it up in the air, I must be going crazy!"

"Let's go for a walk and find Teddy."

We found him on the other side of the tent by himself. She said, "Teddy, we should tell him, now."

Mischa and Teddy took me away from the tent area. I blurted out, "What the hell is going on? This is some weird stuff. OK, this isn't the Moscow Circus. So what kind of a show is this?"

Mischa glanced over at Teddy and he nodded back at her. She took a deep breath and began. "Well, Finn. When the magic show started a few years ago, we met travelers from another planet who were here on Earth and they shared their knowledge with us. We incorporated this into our magic shows. What appears to be magic is actually the technology they gave us. I know this is kind of strange but believe me we all thought that when we first learned this stuff."

I stared at them in open disbelief as Teddy took up the story from there. "Our friends have taught us so many things that seem impossible to believe. Our audiences see it as magic."

"When you look at the introduction of guns and bullets to the Indians in the American West, the natives thought guns were magic fire sticks. When the Aztecs saw the Spaniards arrive in their sailing ships they had no understanding of ships and didn't believe that they really existed. These primitive cultures didn't have any explanation of how guns could shoot bullets or ships could sail across the oceans. It was magic to them."

I responded, "You mean like those small stones. The spinners that Joey was playing with, were NOT a figment of my imagination? They were small devices or something like that?"

Teddy explained, "Joey's bag of stones become whatever he wants them to be. They're actually small machines that respond to voice commands and change to whatever shape he wants them to be. Remember those first video games of the 1970's and how crude they were in the beginning? Then over time they became more and more sophisticated? Well, these are very advanced 3D video games and they have a little more 'kick' to them."

"That's cool!"

Teddy chuckled, "Yes, they are pretty cool. There is still much more to show you but we have to do this in small stages. In this way you will learn to use these skills as we go. Too much and your mind will close and you will not learn anything. When I cup my hands I have this intense strength to blow air through them. It amplifies my lung output. It comes from the biomechanical enhancements that I have. Also you saw how we could raise up the tent, just me and the other gents. We have this ability to push against the planet's gravity. This is all part of the advanced technology our friends have given us."

My head was already swimming with the thoughts of what I'd heard so far when Mischa continued. "One night after a show in my home country of Romania the first magicians met some admirers who came backstage. These were the travelers from another planet."

"They wanted to teach the magicians some very special talents and help them develop more tricks for their show. The magicians were skeptical and wanted to know what the travelers wanted in return. The travelers came to Earth to find a few dozen people who would be willing to join them to start a new world. But first the travelers wanted to make sure what they would teach us would not be abused."

"OK, this is all pretty far-fetched, if you ask me!"

Mischa put her hand on mine, "Finn, you probably

don't remember but Teddy and I met you about six months ago in New Mexico. Unfortunately we could not spend more time with you then. We passed by you on a walking trail at the Petroglyph National Park in Albuquerque. One person in our group asked you if you had seen a young boy who was lost from his mother. You took it upon yourself to run back up the trail to look for Joey. You looked up and down that trail and you helped us eventually find him. We knew then that you were a good person, willing to help us."

Suddenly, it hit me. I remembered helping to find the little boy in the park. So that was Joey!

But her perfume, I remembered that too! That smell that I noticed last night, when she leaned over to talk to me, it was the same smell at the park only a few months ago. The fragrance of those desert flowers, which were in bloom all over the park; that was her smell.

"What was my skill that made you want me in your group?"

"We know that you are a good man. We believe all that you learn you will use wisely. Mischa is a good judge of character. I trust in her senses."

Well, I thought to myself, that settles it. This is all too much for me right now. There may be a plausible

34

explanation for all this magic stuff, but they wanted me to join them. Was this a cult or something? I was wondering what I was getting myself into.

Mischa said, "Finn, we knew you'd be skeptical. We actually hoped you'd not believe at first. That way when you do believe, in your heart, it will be forever!"

"Well, I have to think this over."

I got up and walked over to the bike. I had to go for a ride and sort things out. I looked over at Mischa and Teddy. They looked back and nodded. I got on the bike and started the engine, the twin cylinders purred just like always. What a great sound! I twisted the throttle hand grip and Mischa and Teddy disappeared behind me in the rear view mirror.

I had to get away and think about what they had told me. I needed to get lost on the open road for a while and clear my head of everything else.

# LATER THAT AFTERNOON

I couldn't remember where I went, which roads I took or even if I was on the bike or not. But, a few hours later, I was riding back into camp, surprised to see that everything was set up for tonight's show. All over the tent was something to look at from small flags to posters. The originally drab looking tent was now decked out in a vast array of bright colors.

Jugglers and magicians were walking around the grounds practicing their performances for the show. The younger members of the group were dressed up in cute little costumes as though they came directly out of a

Renaissance Faire.

There was a juggler whose objects were floating in the air and not even touching his hands and yet he was juggling. Weirdness happened once again. Maybe I should just say 'amazing', and leave it at that.

I parked the bike next to Mischa and Teddy's motor home. They must have seen me ride up because the door opened and out came Mischa.

"Finn, you're back. I'm glad you want to stay."

How could she tell? She must have the ability to read minds. I wondered if that meant she could tell what I was thinking about her. I felt my face getting red, very red with embarrassment. I looked at her and she was getting red in the face. Damn, she knows that about me too! We laughed together. What a woman!

Teddy came up behind me. I turned around.

"I take it you're with us?"

"Yes, my friend, I want to be part of your troupe".

"Good then, I think you should be part of tonight's entertainment, as well."

I explained that I couldn't juggle or do tricks.

"That won't be necessary. We have something anyone can do, especially the newest member. Let's say it will be your cup of tea!"

# A PROPER CUP OF TEA

Mischa and I went back to the motor home. She told me she was going to make some tea for us. I told her I was more of a coffee drinker. She looked at me and said, "Please Finn, you need to drink this tea for your performance tonight, trust me."

We sat at the small table and sipped our tea. I thought to myself; I am at a frickin' tea party. Yeah, with the most beautiful woman I've ever seen...she's so pretty. Oh, oh, I was getting stoned. What the heck did she put in my tea? I felt like the room was spinning around and I noticed she was getting a little wobbly too.

She touched my hand. Our two hands felt strange. I looked down at our hands and we were wearing some kind of rubber gloves like the ones you wear when you're washing dishes. Mine were green and hers were a lovely shade of pink. I really loved that color on her. I started to tell her that I loved her shade of pink.

Mischa suggested, "Just stay calm. You're going to have fun, I promise. I should have told you more about what is going to happen."

I started to panic. "WHAT IS GOING TO HAPPEN?"

"Don't worry, my love. You're going to have fun. You'll be fine."

When she said that I thought, "She called me 'my love'...that's so wonderful. She loves me." Her soothing voice calmed me down.

We finished the rest of the tea and by now I felt myself really lightheaded, actually, my whole body felt lightheaded. Oh, oh, I felt like I was a helium balloon. I was facing Mischa, or I thought it was Mischa. I was face to face looking at someone in the strangest spacesuit I'd ever seen.

"Mischa, is that you?"

"Yes, dear, it's me."

Why was she in a spacesuit? And why was she

floating? She was kinda bouncing from floor to ceiling. But wait a minute, so was I. I was in some kind of a spacesuit. It was green like the rubber gloves I had on my hands, but it now covered my whole body. I had a clear section over my face, just like Mischa had and yet I was breathing and it was cool inside. I thought this must be what astronauts have in their space suits. So this weird, err, amazing suit had some sort of cooling system. It was OK by me!

Mischa said that we need to focus on what we were going to do in the show. I thought, "Man! That was some potent tea!" Just then the motor home door opened and Teddy poked his head inside and asked Mischa if we were ready.

"Ready for what?" I thought. "What am I doing here?" I certainly was stoned.

"Finn, we're going for a Moon Walk on Earth."

"Oh, great!" I wasn't too sure what that meant, but I figured if she was there with me, I couldn't get into too much trouble!

"It will be OK, I promise. Let's go." Mischa calmed my anxiety once again.

# IN THE TENT

Mischa and I walked from the motor home to the rear of the tent. I was enjoying the bounce in my step while wearing this spacesuit. I glanced over at Mischa. She was bouncing as she was walking too! This made me feel like a kid again. I was really having a good time.

Teddy stood at the opening in the back of the tent and waved at us to come to him. Once inside the tent we saw a bench and he directed us to sit down. We were separated from the main area by a curtain.

Teddy stood in front of us and explained what we were going to do for our performance. I sensed he was talking mainly to me, as Mischa had probably done this many times before.

"You will fly around in the tent and perform acrobatics with the music. The other people in our group will help you and guide you with your stunts."

I thought, "Acrobatics! Now that's going to be funny." I started to giggle. I looked over at Mischa and she was giggling too! She knew why I was laughing.

I thought about that time in high school gym class when we were learning acrobatics and gymnastics. Our principal heard from our gym teacher that we were doing a great job in the class performing the various routines. The principal thought we should perform for the School District Superintendent the following week.

So, a week later in front of the entire school and the District Superintendent we performed our entire routine of moves just like a 'well-oiled machine'. It was stunning, if I say so myself. Everything was coming together just perfectly, right up to the final number when I was going to pick up Julie and toss her up in the air. I was standing right in front of the school officials as I knelt down to pick up Julie. She was just a little heavier than I expected. I was supposed to toss her in the air. The music in the background was playing louder and louder. It was building in intensity and just then it stopped. I think this was to make sure that everyone was watching us.

I went down on one knee to put myself in the proper position to pick her up. Then when I started to lift her up I *farted*...oh, jeez, it was awful. It was loud; the sound reverberated throughout the gymnasium. All the students, all the teachers, all the staff, the District Superintendent and Julie will forever have that image etched in their minds. I would always be the boy who has just totally embarrassed himself in front of three hundred people.

I remember seeing every mouth wide open. No one knew what to say, what to think or how to act after this unmentionable event had happened. I started to laugh. Then another person laughed. Then the whole gymnasium laughed. It was the funniest thing that had ever happened in our school. So for the rest of the year, I was called all kinds of things, but mostly people laughed. We all really enjoyed the silliness of the whole thing. Needless to say, I never performed in front of any large group again.

This was going through my mind and I couldn't help but feel worried that I might do this again. All of a sudden I heard Mischa's voice in my head telling me not to worry. Holy Cow, not only can she read my thoughts, but she can talk to me too! She said that while I was in the suit and even if I exploded a bomb inside the suit, no one would know what I had done. That made me feel better until I thought, "OK, this suit is pretty strong and I didn't notice any zipper. So how did I get into this suit and how do I get out of it?" Mischa said I would know in due time and not to worry. Somehow, I figured she'd say that. I let it go and tried to return to listening to Teddy.

He told me just to watch Mischa and do what she does. He said I should face her and let the other members of the group guide me. The other folks in the group would be running the show.

"Just have fun."

"Yeah, right!"

Even though I was not in a mood to worry I had no idea what I was doing and that made me feel uneasy. So Mischa stood up and took me by the hand. We walked from the small room to the main part of the arena. We could now see what was happening in front of the crowd. The entertainers were withdrawing from the open area and exiting behind us. Mischa was whispering reassurances in my mind as we entered.

# THE FINAL ACT

Teddy walked out to the audience and said, "Ladies and Gentlemen!  For our final act, we are now going to show you a gravity-defying presentation. We guarantee that you will be amazed. I would like to leave you with one last thought. Magic comes in all forms in life. We came to entertain you and wish that you leave with a smile on your face and a desire to share the magic in life with others around you."

"Ladies and Gentlemen! Boys and Girls! Without wires, just the magic of their suits and their own skills, here are Mischa and Finn."

The music came up louder. The spot lights were focused on us. The other entertainers came up and led us to the front of the crowd. Mischa waved to the crowd. I waved too, just copying whatever Mischa did.

Raising my arm I noticed my suit. The color was glowing a lime-green shade and then became brighter to a more yellowish shade. I realized the suit was pulsating colors in time to my heartbeats. OK, that was weird. I looked over at Mischa. Her suit was displaying a vivid pinkish color and also vibrating in time to her heartbeats. How did these suits do that?

I tipped my head down to look at the ground moving away from me. I was being lifted in the air by the others, just like Mischa. They pointed us over the heads of the audience and let us go. We were like  helium balloons and it was a wonderful feeling, just floating along. I noticed that I could steer myself by thinking about where I wanted to go. Children below were jumping up trying to touch us. I was floating just a few feet above the crowd. I could see the wonder in their eyes, young and old, everyone was focused on what we were doing.

I was having a lot of fun and I felt like I was the star of the show, along with Mischa, of course! Then the colors of our suits seemed to change once again. This time the colors were in beat to the music and stuff started to come out of our suits. There were little things like shooting stars, small fireworks, all kinds of stuff. I looked over at Mischa. She was floating over the audience. Small candies were coming out of her hands and dropping to the children below. I waved my hands and I too was also throwing candies from my hands and shooting off fireworks.

It was a wonderful show. The crowd clapped their hands, stomped their feet and shouted for us to keep going. Mischa and I flew around the crowd until she motioned for me to hold her hands. We grabbed one another and started to spin around above the audience. We began spinning faster and faster and then BLAM! Both Mischa and I found ourselves in the small area off-stage. We were somehow out of our suits and we could hear the crowd clapping.

We ran back into the main area. Teddy welcomed us back. The spotlight was shining brightly on both of us. We took a bow, turned and headed out of the arena.

Teddy told the audience, "Ladies and gentlemen, boys and girls. We hope you have had as much fun seeing the show as we've had bringing it to you. Go with the joy of the magic of the night. Good Night!"

# INTO THE NIGHT

Mischa gave me a hug and thanked me for a great performance. I told her this was one of the happiest times of my life. I thought, "It's really cool to be entertaining people and to be with you!"

"Finn, this was very special for me too!"

Teddy came up to us as we were leaving the tent. "You chaps did a great job. Everyone has been telling me what a wonderful show it's been. Well done!"

Mischa invited me into the motor home for a glass of wine. I opened the motor home door and held it open as I bowed and said, "Madam, please enter." She stuck out her hand like a lady of the court. I held her hand and escorted her inside. We laughed.

I had to ask Mischa not to give me anything as powerful as the tea we had earlier in the day. I told her this mentally, as we were only using telepathy to communicate now. I was surprised that I could communicate with her without speaking. I was beginning to like these new skills I had.

"Yes, that was some pretty strong tea we had earlier. I'm sure you've never had that kind of tea before. And now Finn, I have a story to tell you. I want you to know about me."

She poured two glasses of wine and set the bottle to the side. I looked into her eyes. We held each other's hands as she began her story.

# MISCHA'S STORY

I was born in Romania, a poor country, but growing up poor does not mean you cannot be happy. Until Mama died we had a loving little family. It happened so quickly. First, Mama was sick and then a few weeks after the doctors told us it was stomach cancer and she passed away.

She died when I was fifteen years old and Dasha, my sister, was only thirteen. Losing her was something that we never spoke about but I still think about her every day of my life.

Mama and Papa really loved each other. They never

argued or disagreed. The other parents that we knew did not have a relationship like our Mama and Papa. When we were outside walking to the park or to the store, they would just talk quietly with each other, not like other families where the father would rule the household by shouting and commanding the mother and children to do his bidding. The love between our parents was something that Dasha and I knew was very strong and built on respect for one another. We missed her in our lives terribly.

What was very interesting was that right after Mama died, Dasha, my younger sister, became the mother of the family. She became assertive, helping Papa and me, comforting us, telling us what to do. She was the strong one to be sure. She inherited Mama's strong spirit even at her young age!

Papa had a good job working for the city, as a maintenance worker. He could keep all kinds of things working with just simple tools and a keen eye for fixing things. But when the Great Depression came he lost his job and like so many other innocent people in our country he was without work. Providing for our family became a challenge for him but fortunately not for long.

Papa was resourceful and because he could fix things,

many neighbors and friends of our neighbors would come to our flat and ask Papa to look at their broken toasters and radios and even their cars. After just a short time Papa's skill became the saving grace for our family and he got quite a reputation around town. He could fix almost anything that he was given and he would never give a bill. He'd let people pay whatever they could afford. People would be so appreciative that they would always give us food or clothes or furniture.

Once I remembered him at our front door talking to a forlorn looking old woman who had brought something that had broken down. He invited her into our flat and she sat next to him at the kitchen table while he took a look at what she had brought. She sat there without taking off her grey coat and hat. She watched Papa fiddle with a screwdriver and pliers and within a few minutes, he gave it back to our guest and proclaimed it fixed. The very grateful woman promised to return with something to thank him for his labor. When she did return a short time later she had with her a sack of vegetables and fresh fruit.

This was a regular occurrence with the people that Papa helped. For all these people he would brush off their offers of payment, saying he was happy to fix this or that for them. But in a short time we'd have a dozen of eggs, a few loaves of bread, some wine or some other token of their thanks, and we never went hungry. As Dasha and I would see how Papa treated people and the way they gave us food and other things, we felt very proud that he could keep us warm, fed and relatively happy even though times were tough and even though he didn't have a job. We didn't know how quickly this life would change.

# OUR WORST DAY EVER

One day, when I was seventeen years old, I was walking home from school. I was thinking about how much homework I had to do that night and I had to fix dinner and help Dasha with her lessons. Then I heard a voice behind me saying, "Mischa! Mischa!" I turned around. It was Peter, a classmate in my school.

Peter was not a nice person. He would bully people and say very bad things to the teachers. He would argue with any authority figure who told him what to do.

"I like you Mischa. I want to go out with you."

I told him that I was not allowed to see him. "You are

mean to people. I will never go out with you as long as you are like this."

"What are you saying, silly girl! It's a tough world now, or hasn't anyone told you! Look, you won't do any better out there with any of the other boys. You should be <u>MY</u> girl friend."

"Peter, you can't succeed in life by being a bully. I'm going to work hard and do well in school. You should too!"

He grabbed me and tried to kiss me but I was able to turn my head and prevent his lips from touching mine.

"Don't fight me, Mischa. I want you and if I can't have you, no one else will either."

I turned away and ran home. I didn't look back to see if he was following me. I ran to the elevator and kept pushing the elevator button. Finally it arrived and the doors opened. I ran inside, the doors closed and I pushed the button for my floor. I was safe but shaking. I was terrified of Peter. Rumor had it he sold drugs and always carried a gun with him, one rumor I was sure to be true.

When I entered our flat and came into the kitchen, Papa was at the kitchen table working on some appliance. He looked up at me and saw I was crying. "What is wrong, my Mischa?"

I couldn't stop crying, "Papa, it is that boy, Peter. He has said things. He wants to have me as his girlfriend. I don't like him. He is a bad person. He's mean to the other students, to the teachers, and I don't like him. I am very afraid of him."

Papa hugged me and said, "There now, little one. If he comes here I will have a talk with him. We must be reasonable. Get your sister. Let's have some dinner. One of my friends has brought us a nice roast. We will have a good dinner."

Even when things were going badly, Papa could always see the positive side in life and tried to make the negative go away. But somehow I knew this wasn't going to get much better. I entered our bedroom to tell Dasha it was time for dinner.

"So Peter is bothering you."

"How do you know this?"

"He's been telling everyone at school that he wants you to be his girl friend no matter what it takes. He's a scary person. Be careful."

Just then the doorbell rang, Dasha and I came out of our room and we saw Papa open the front door. Peter was there at the door and shouting at Papa, "Get that girl out here old man. I want to talk to her. No girl ever runs away from me!"

Papa tried to calm Peter down and invited him into our flat. Peter saw me standing behind Papa. Peter pulled a small black pistol from his pocket and pointed it at me. Papa tried to take the gun from Peter's hand but Peter was holding steady on the handle of the gun. Papa couldn't get it away from him. Peter and Papa were both trying to pull the gun out of the other's hand. Dasha and I screamed at Papa to be careful. There was a loud BANG, a puff of smoke and Papa was knocked backwards and fell to the floor.

Dasha and I rushed to Papa who was now on the floor and bleeding from his chest.

"You made me do that, Mischa."

Dasha and I looked at Peter. He ran to the stairs at the end of the hallway and down the stairwell. Dasha and I knelt down next to our Papa, who was dying in our arms. He was breathing heavily and gasping for air. Dasha and I were crying and screaming.

Our neighbors came running from the other flats. Someone must have called for the police and an ambulance, as they arrived within a few minutes. Then someone took us away from Papa and the medics put him on the gurney and covered him with a sheet. And at that moment, the world that we knew was taken from us.

A few days later Papa was buried. A very kind couple, Josef and Sophia, came to our flat and told us what we had already known. If we did not have any family we would be placed in a special home for abandoned children. Of course, we did not want that and Josef and Sophia invited us to come and live with them. They told us we would be safe with them.

Josef and Sophia were the leaders of a small group of magicians who put on magic shows. The members of the troupe lived together in a building in the old industrial part of town and what they offered us would be a home and a family.

Dasha and I talked about it later that evening and decided that was what we should do. We both cried until we had no more tears left. We were crying for Mama, for Papa, and for ourselves.

The next day Josef and Sophia helped us leave our flat and move what few belongings we had. They gave us our own little room; two beds, two small dressers, a clothes closet and a small black stove. Once we were settled in our room, Dasha and I looked at each other and cried. It sank in that this was going to be our new home.

# THIS STRANGE BUILDING

We moved to the industrial area of our city. Our building stood out from all the others. It was built from very dark, stained wood, whereas the other buildings in this area were made of concrete and construction bricks from the Communist era. Compared to the concrete buildings ours was small with only three stories.

I realized that all of the other buildings were either empty or abandoned. There was no bustle of people from these buildings. Their windows were all boarded up, making the surrounding area feel lifeless. Fortunately, our building was more than occupied. The lower floor was where the magic shows were performed so it was very populated during the shows.

That left the second floor for the kitchen and storage. The third floor was where all the bedrooms were located.

I never thought about it then but now I realize this was a very strange building. On the inside of the building was a ramp but no stairs. If you took it in one direction you could walk to all the floors, first floor to the second floor to the third floor and then if you walked a little bit more you would be back to the first floor, without going downhill! I don't know how this was done, but it worked.

Sometimes in our room at night we would hear a crackling sound and for a second I would see our heater change shape. One minute it was a heater then the next minute it would look different, but only for a second or two. I thought I was seeing things because I was tired. But something *was* going on that was strange.

For the first week we were there, Dasha and I spent most of the time in our room consoling each other. But our mourning period ended when Josef and Sophia asked us to be part of the magic show that evening. Dasha didn't need to be asked twice. She was ready to start living again. I was still feeling much remorse and uncertainty about our future, but I followed her lead. We promised to leave our room and attend that evening's performance. We didn't know that Josef and Sophia had a big surprise in store for us!

# OUR FIRST PERFORMANCE AND A NEW LIFE

As we were having our afternoon meal with the others in our group, Sophia gave us both cups of tea. She said, "This tea's a special blend to help you perform this evening. Enjoy ladies!"

I looked at Dasha and we both raised our eyebrows wondering what she meant. Sophia then placed two cups of dark tea in front of us, gave us a wink and quickly turned around and went back to serving the others and trusting us to drink it.

"What did she say that we are going to perform? Do you think we should drink this? Dasha can we trust this? I mean it's all so strange."

"Oh, sure!" Dasha responded with a smile; one that was not quite convincing me. I couldn't help wondering if this was the right thing to do.

I stared at the tea for some time. The aroma of the tea was sweet and inviting. We sipped the hot tea and in a few minutes, Dasha and I were feeling wonderful. Our inhibitions were taking a back seat to our thoughts which were running wild. I began to wonder what we would be performing in this evening's show.

After we drank our tea, Josef came to our table and told us we would be helping the other performers; a disappearing act and a special display of magic - flying above the audience. He smiled as he told us that tonight was our first look at being able to do magic, to experience how it felt. Dasha and I looked at each other and smiled.

Sophia came back to our table and announced, "Girls, I have placed costumes on your beds for you to change into." Sophia motioned for us to clean up our table and get ready. "Off to your room. Then come down when you've changed."

We saw two shimmering outfits laid out, one on each of our beds. They were made with some kind of shiny material that seemed luxurious. Both of these costumes had been laid out in such a way that it looked like two people were asleep on our beds except there was no head, hands or feet. Dasha's costume was red with small stars. My suit was the same style except that it was blue.

As I touched my costume, I felt a tingling in the material, just a little shock like static electricity or something. Dasha must have felt the same thing as she let out a little "Yip!" We both laughed and agreed that it must be static electricity in the air.

When we performed that evening we were able to do some very special tricks while we wore these costumes. It was exhilarating being able to fly, to go the direction we wanted on a whim. We enjoyed being a part of the troupe and doing magic like this in front of an audience.

You see for Dasha and me, this was a whole new beginning in our lives. Dasha and I were having fun with our new family, learning how to do these tricks for our audience and not having any more worries. We didn't know how long this would last.

Unfortunately about a year later, one night during a typical show, we were jolted out of our dream world. Everything changed once again.

# ONE DOOR CLOSES

One night as the audience was enjoying our show there was a commotion from the back of the theater. We heard Josef plead, "Please don't go in there! We are performing for the audience!" Josef was pushed aside by a group of young men carrying guns.

I flew above the crowd and quickly caught Dasha's attention. She signaled for us to land and to see what was going on. One of the young robbers had a gun in his hand. It was Peter, the same young man who shot and killed my father. He ordered his gang to take everything valuable from us. They were robbing us!

# ONCE UPON A MAGIC NIGHT

Anger overtook my fear and I landed just a few feet away from Peter. I was trembling but I demanded that he stop what he was doing this instant and leave immediately. I told him we would call the police.

He laughed and said there was nothing we could do to stop him. That was when he recognized me. He said, "Ah, my sweet Mischa! I've been looking for you, so this is where you ran to. You were foolish to try to get away from me. Now that your father is not here, I can finally have you."

We were forced into the backstage room by the gang members. Peter pointed his gun at us and told us to sit down on the floor. Josef begged Peter to release us. If they would to let us go he would show them where more money was kept. Peter looked at his gang and ordered them to stay here with the women. Then he pushed his gun into Josef's ribs and told him to show him where the money was.

Josef said, "No, let Mischa and Dasha go. Then I will show you where the money is kept." Josef turned to his wife and they traded strange looks. It was like they were talking to each other. I turned to Dasha who looked back at me and we both shrugged our shoulders. We were terrified and there was no way to know what Josef and

Sophia were going to do next.

Peter walked up to me and pulled me up from the floor by my hair. I screamed for him to stop. Sophia lunged towards me faster than I thought anyone could move, especially an old woman. Josef ran just as quickly towards the other bullies in the room. For a second I thought to myself, God, I don't want anything to happen to my friends. Please don't let them get hurt.

I looked at Peter; he raised his gun and aimed it at Sophia. She held up her hands to her mouth and she blew air through her hands in Peter's direction. BLAM, a powerful gust of wind hit Peter throwing him backwards against the far wall. He hit the wall so hard that he dropped his gun but not before it went off, the bullet headed straight towards Sophia.

I screamed, "NO..." and watched in amazement as Sophia reached up with her hand and caught the bullet in mid-air. She closed her fist around it and dropped it harmlessly on the ground.

My God, what is going on here? I turned towards Peter, who was lying still on the floor. His head was bleeding where it had made contact with the wall. It looked like he was knocked out.

Josef grabbed both of the other two bullies and

knocked their heads together with such a cracking sound that it made me sick to my stomach. The bullies fell lifeless to the floor.

Dasha came over to me now that we were free from these mad men. Tears of relief were streaming down our faces. Josef and Sophia ran over to us and hugged us. Sophia checked us over to make sure we weren't hurt. She nodded to Josef. "Darlings, we're so glad you are alright."

Josef turned his head to Sophia as though he was talking to her but his lips weren't moving. She nodded at Josef. Then I knew. They were telepaths.

Sophia told us to stay behind them as we reentered the main theater area. The rest of the gang was in the center of the theater with a pile of money, wallets, watches and things that they had taken so far. They were so intent on counting their stolen treasure, they didn't pay any attention to us walking up behind them.

Then one of them must have seen us out of the corner of his eye and turned towards us shouting, "Stop! Where is Peter? Where are the other guys?"

Josef laughed, telling them, "Peter and the other guys fought us and lost. Just like what is going to happen to you!"

# ONCE UPON A MAGIC NIGHT

The boys scrambled to their feet grabbing their guns and pointed them at us. We walked closer to where the boys were standing. They fired their guns at us. Bullets left the barrels of the guns through clouds of smoke followed by a deep thud and blast of light. Sophia and Josef moved quickly in front of the guns and grabbed the bullets before they could hit anyone.

The expressions of the boys' faces were priceless. They should have come to the magic show rather than try to rob us. Then they wouldn't have been so surprised to see what was going to happen next.

Josef and Sophia moved in unison, both raised their outstretched arms and pointed their cupped hands at the boys and puffs of air came from their mouths directly at each boy's chest. BLAM-BLAM! Each boy was hit so hard with these sonic waves that you could hear their ribs crack. They must have felt excruciating pain directly to their hearts. Each one fell to the floor with the look of complete surprise on their faces.

With all this going on I didn't see Peter come up behind me. He put his hand on my throat and squeezed hard. I couldn't breathe and I felt a knife in my side. I tried to scream for help but he had such a tight grip on my throat I couldn't make a sound.

Peter whispered in my ear, "I've told you that if I couldn't have you, no one else would either!"

I tried again to cry for help but again this was in vain. Dasha saw what was happening and she jumped at Peter and punched him in the head. I heard the thump of her fist hitting his head. He let go of me and I was able to breathe again. Peter staggered and caught himself before falling over. He lunged at Dasha with knife in hand. This was all happening so fast.

She screamed in pain, "MISCHA!" The knife had hit its mark.

I screamed, "DASHA!"

Josef flew through the air and landed on Peter's back and shook him off Dasha. Josef picked Peter up and carried him up through the air up to the ceiling, about 20 feet or so. He threw Peter down to the ground. Peter hit the floor with a loud crash and was totally lifeless. This time there was no doubt that Peter was not getting up again. He looked like a limp rag doll with legs and arms akimbo.

I crawled over and held my sweet sister in my arms gently stroking her hair and begging her to stay with me. She looked up at me as she coughed and gave up her last breath. Sophia and Josef both hugged us. I screamed in anguish, "NO, NO. GOD, NO!" sobbing over my sister who gave up her life trying to save me! Now I had no one left in my family, my mother, my father, my sister, all gone. Now I really was an orphan. Sophia and Josef hugged me very tightly. I couldn't stop holding on to my sister.

When the police came by to write up their report they told me that Dasha was very brave to try to protect me. They had been after this gang for a long time. Now the city wouldn't have these criminals around because of our bravery. The police told us that we were all heroes, especially Dasha, who had given her life.

# BACK IN THE TRAILER

Mischa poured the last bit of wine into my glass. I thought to her, "Wow! What a story! You have had an incredibly hard life. I'm so sorry for your losses, your father and your sister in such a short time. Yet, I'm thankful you have found your new family."

I held Mischa's hands in mine and we drew close to one another. I started to kiss her, when just then there was a loud pounding on the door of the motor home. BAM-BAM-BAM. A woman's voice shouted, "Mischa! Finn! Are you in there? Open up! They've taken Joey and now Teddy is missing!"

Mischa and I jumped up and answered the door, our hearts racing. It was Sophie. In a frantic voice, she told us that right after the show, she turned around to get Joey and he was gone. She saw Teddy and asked him to help look for her son. Teddy told her that he saw the two rednecks hanging around the back of the tent where Joey was last seen. Sophie started to cry. Now Teddy was missing also.

I looked at Mischa and I thought to her, "You stay here with Sophie. I think I know where they are. I'll go get them. Keep everyone else together until I return."

Mischa told me telepathically, "Please, you be careful. I don't know what I'd do without you!" I kissed her on the cheek, nodded to her and Sophie and left.

# THE ENCOUNTER

I got on the Triumph. One kick, a twist of the throttle and off I went. I quickly got on the road and headed through town. I rode in the direction of where I remembered I had seen the red-necks' truck in front of a small house just outside of town when I came here yesterday.

As I was riding the bike, I thought about wearing leather boots. Then something weird happened, my shoes turned into leather boots. They weren't normal leather boots, they were shinier, blacker and stronger than what I liked for leather riding boots. My feet felt energized by them like I had on running shoes that looked and felt like boots. Damn, I thought. This is good! I was happy that some of the cool stuff from the flying suit was still in my body.

As the last buildings of town faded behind me, I tried to figure how many miles I had to go before I reached the house. Five miles, seven miles, it couldn't be much farther. The sagebrush and small cacti were the only other things to look at on the side of the road. There was a full moon over the desert. If you have never seen a sight like this, you really need to. It is a sight to behold. The black sky with the stars and the clouds is so beautiful. The air is so clear. The shadows of the plants on the ground make you think it could be daytime!

I was trying to keep my mind on what I was doing and trying not to just daydream about everything that had happened to me. I had only met these people yesterday and yet, I really liked them. And now I was putting myself on the line for them. Was I sure I wanted to do this? What was I thinking? I liked these people and I could see myself getting closer to Mischa. I hadn't felt this way about anyone in a very long time. Could I keep drifting through life or was this what I was looking for? Yes, damn it. This is what I've been searching for.

## OnCE UPOn A MAGIC NIGHT

For all the right reasons, I had to help these people. What with my Army training and those missions I'd been on, I knew I was prepared for a fight, whenever necessary. I couldn't stop thinking about that boy who had died on my last mission before I was discharged from the Army. I had been running from situations since that boy died. I felt I was personally responsible for his death. I had to stand up for these people. I had to face my demons.

I needed a plan. What was I to do? I couldn't waltz up to the front door of the house and just ask for my friends back. No, I had to have a distraction, get them to lose their focus and that should give me the advantage I needed to rescue my friends.

The road rose up over a small hill and then descended down the other side of the next valley where I could see a house in the distance. This was the house I was looking for. I found myself wishing that I could see the house better and just as I thought it, my eyes suddenly focused on the house as if I had held a set of binoculars. Man, these enhancements to my body were really coming in handy.

I slowed the motorcycle down, shut off the engine and coasted to a stop. I could see the lights inside the house were on and the red-neck truck was parked in front. It was a shabby looking house and there was garbage strewn all around front and back. There were a couple of junked cars on blocks that were partially dismantled on the side of the house. What a dump!

I parked the bike behind the truck where I thought no one in the house would see me. I got off the bike and walked around their truck. I was trying to be as quiet as possible when I realized that I wasn't really walking on the ground. My feet were a few inches above the dirt. Jeez, I was floating toward the house. This was perfect!

As I got closer to the house, I started to recon the situation. Good old Army training! I was ready to go around to the back of the house when front door burst open.

One of the red necks shouted, "Hey, boy! We figured somebody would be comin' so we kept a look out for ya'. We got your friends in here. We want to know where they got their strength from. They ain't tellin' us nothin'."

"I don't care what you want. I'm gonna kick your asses. You better let my friends go and save yourself a lot of trouble and bloodshed!"

"If there's any blood gonna be spilt, it's gonna be yours."

# ONCE UPON A MAGIC NIGHT

I thought for a second that this conversation sounded like a bad western. Just then a bullet came whizzing over my head and hit a cactus behind me splitting it into a hundred pieces. I ducked down behind the back of the truck and tried to think about what to do next.

I looked up and was surprised to see the rednecks on each side of me. They had boxed me in and they were pointing their guns at me. I had to give up. I was outflanked and surrendering now was my only option. I stood up with my hands in the air, not knowing what else to do.

Then it hit me, I'm wearing the super-suit. I could just think about what I wanted to do and the suit would do it. So I thought about flying up in the air. I took off straight up and looked down at the two red-necks with very surprised looks on their puffy, drunken faces. I hovered in the air trying to figure out what to do next, when the drunken bastards started shooting at me.

I dove downward and flew into the open doorway of the house. I thought if I had a burst of speed, I could grab Joey and get him out of the house to safety. And if my luck held, I could make a second pass and get Teddy. I saw both Joey and Teddy tied up in the living room. Teddy didn't look like he was completely conscious, his head was nodding from side to side and his eyes were half open.

Joey had his mouth taped shut so he couldn't talk, but as soon as he saw me he was making noises. I tried to tell him to shush by putting my index finger over my lips, but he didn't listen and continued making noises. I desperately wanted to get my friends out of this house before the red-necks got back inside.

Whatever they had given him, Teddy was really out of it. I tried shaking him but I couldn't get him to focus on me. I turned around right as the two good ol' boys walked in and pointed their guns at me.

I thought I needed a shield or something to defend myself in case they shot at me or Joey or Teddy. As I was visualizing this, I felt a hardened plate over my chest that could have been a protective vest. I sure hoped it was bullet-proof. I didn't really want to ask the red-necks to try shooting me to see if this worked.

Without any hesitation I grabbed Joey and tried to protect him as much as possible by keeping him on the side away from the red necks. I turned to look for Teddy, when something struck my head. I dropped to my knees. Everything went dark. I must have been knocked out.

When I came to both of the red-necks were standing

over me and I was handcuffed. My head hurt like hell and Teddy and Joey were not in the same room with me.

I demanded answers, "Where are you keeping Teddy and Joey? Why are you doing this? Why are you holding us hostage?"

They laughed and one of them said, "You sure are a stupid boy, ain't ya'? Ha! We want you to learn us all your fancy magic tricks. Hell, with tricks like that we could rob whenever we want and...and get away with it all! Show us your tricks boy and we'll let you go."

I answered back, "I'll never show you anything! I don't even know <u>how </u>they do it. I've only known them for two days. They haven't bothered you. You call me stupid. Did you ever stop to think if you had asked them nicely, maybe they would have shown you?"

They laughed. One of the red-necks said, "Bring her in."

I thought her who? My mind was racing; who was he talking about? He left the room and he came back with Mischa. Her mouth had been taped shut and her hands were tied together. She seemed to be groggy just like Teddy. Damn, why did she come here? I had told her to stay with Sophie at the camp. Can she read my thoughts now? I hoped she would talk to me telepathically. But nothing, I wasn't hearing anything from her.

I pleaded with these guys, "Let them go and I'll show you how the magic suit works, just let them all go. Once they are gone I'll teach you everything."

Then the red-necks laughed and one of them said, "Well, we'll just see boy, after we have our way with her, or maybe after we take care of the King of England here."

One of the red-necks was holding Mischa while the other one pointed his gun at her from the other side of the room. He pulled the trigger and fired at Mischa.

For a moment, I was back in the Army trying to rescue that young Afghan boy. I knew he was going to stand up, but now this time I could change the outcome. This time I was able to pull him down and save him from being shot. Then I found myself back in the present.

I found myself flying through the room. All my thoughts focused on stopping that bullet. I had to be a human shield for this woman I cared for.

For a second I thought I heard her say, "Thanks, Finn." But this was probably just a whisper that I imaged her saying as she was still too drugged to communicate to me.

The bullet left the barrel of the gun in a flash of light and dull bang. Still in slow motion, I jumped towards the advancing bullet that was approaching my dear sweet Mischa. I had to get in the way of that bullet.

I had to try this desperate act, Mischa was helpless. I had to do something. The red necks sat grinning like the fools they were, happy with themselves as they watched me jump to intercept these bullets.

I anticipated the force of the bullet striking my vest and knocking me backwards. But it was the weirdest feeling. There was absolutely no impact from the bullet. I know the bullet struck my chest but I didn't feel anything. I thought, DAMN, is this what it was like to feel death? Maybe the bullet came through the vest and I was dead! But then the two red-necks grabbed me and stood me up.

I looked down at my chest where I should have seen the impact of the bullet. I saw nothing, no bullet marks, nothing! I didn't know what to think and I couldn't say anything, except, "What the hell?"

# WHEN EVERYTHING CHANGED

Mischa stood up, her hands were now free. The red-neck goons and Teddy smiled at me. They gave me the warmest smiles I had ever seen, well next to Mischa's, of course. Then the red-necks faced each other, and they said together with one voice, "Program over!" and disappeared.

Mischa's telepathic powers were back and she started communicating with me again, "Finn, are you alright?"

"Yeah, so what was this anyway? Was it some kind of a computer game?

Before Mischa could answer me, little Joey and his

mother, Sophie, came into the room and stood next to Mischa. I watched in amazement as Joey started getting taller. He had grey hair and looked to be in his sixties. Sophie got older too and she had white shoulder length hair and held Joey's hand.

I'm sure they all could see the puzzled look on my face. Mischa asked me if I remembered her telling me about the older couple, Josef and Sophia. Of course, I remembered the story. It was only a few hours ago that I heard it.

"Well," she said, "I want you to meet my good friends, Josef and Sophia. Little Joey is actually Josef, my father's friend and this is his wife Sophia. They are our friends who have shared their wonderful technology with us."

Mischa apologized as she told me that this was all a test. They knew that my last Army experience had traumatized me. They needed to make sure I could get past the unfortunate death of that young boy that bothered me so much. It was a test that only I could take.

They wanted to see if I could prove myself if it came to a fight. They said I passed with flying colors. For a second I was a little upset that they had to do it this way. I was so relieved that they were not in danger anymore.

But what a way to test me!

I looked around the room at Teddy, Josef, Sophia, and Mischa. The floor started to vibrate and tilt from side to side and I realized that we were all leaning a little bit.

Josef said, "We are taking off. This is one of our transport ships. We're flying back to our Mother ship which is just outside the solar system. We made this transport vehicle look like a house, but now it's in its true form; an interplanetary flying ship. The others in our magic group have already arrived."

Two seats came out of the floor in front of a command console with a lot of switches and dials. Two view screens came out from the walls showing the transport ship moving away from the Earth below.

Josef and Teddy sat down on the seats and took control of the ship. Sophia sat down next to me and said, "Josef and I are the travelers. We are all that is left from our world, which was similar to Earth but with an old sun that died as we were leaving. We've been travelling the universe for three hundred years searching for people like you and Mischa and Teddy."

I stuttered, "So, so, you and Josef are over three hundred years old?"

"Yes!" she answered, "I'm well over three hundred.

I'm three hundred and fifty seven years old to be exact. I have probably another one hundred and fifty to go. But, Finn, we have a lot to teach you and the others. It will make your lives better."

I turned to Mischa. I told her that it finally hit me. Everything I was looking for was right here. I held her hands in mine.

"You were what we, and," she corrected herself, "*I*, was looking for. And now we're on our way to our new home across the universe. You're not mad at us for doing this?"

"Of course not, I feel like you gave me my life back. I didn't have much left on Earth. The only thing I'm going to miss is my old Triumph motorcycle. But you probably knew that already."

"I have a special present for you. Before we took off, we placed your motorcycle in the house, so you will be able to enjoy it when we get to our new home. I could never want to take anything from you Finn. Especially something that means so much to you."

I looked into her eyes and I held her close and started to kiss her, but all of a sudden I felt dizzy once again. I pulled my head back and shook my head. I closed my eyes.

When I opened my eyes again, I was staring directly into Mischa's eyes, but something was different. I looked around the room. I wasn't in the house anymore. I was sitting at the table in the coffee shop in that little town on the edge of the Mohave Desert.

The waitress came up to our table and asked what my guests would like to have. They ordered two cups of coffee and pie to go with it.

I shook my head, "What just happened?"

But before I got an answer, one of Teddy's comrades came up to our table and said, "Sorry to bother you Teddy but it looks like someone is trying to get into your motor home!"

Teddy replied, "Thanks. I'll take care of it. Finn, would you care to come along?"

I paused for a second and said, "I wouldn't miss this for the world."

81652242R00050

Made in the USA
Columbia, SC
25 November 2017